That morning Peter's class watched a programme about pandas on television. When the programme was finished the teacher asked them all to draw a picture of a panda.

When Peter opened his pencil box to get out his
pencil, he couldn't find it. It wasn't there. His new
pencil was missing.

He called out to tell his teacher, but she was busy helping someone else.

Peter went over to his teacher and pulled her skirt and told her again.

The teacher told him there were some more pencils on her table. But he didn't want one of those. He wanted his new pencil.

Peter went back to his place again and looked inside
his pencil box. It was still empty. He stared at the
piece of paper in front of him and called out again.

The little girl next to Peter was trying to get on with her picture and told him to be quiet.

Peter was cross, he didn't want to be quiet. He pulled her hair.

The teacher came over to see what was going on.
One of the children pointed at Peter.

Peter pulled his hair too. The teacher asked Peter to come with her and told the other children to get on with their work.

Peter started to cry. He told the teacher he couldn't do his picture because he hadn't got a pencil. He wanted his own new pencil.

The teacher gave him a tissue to dry his eyes with and told him not to cry. She told him to look for his pencil at home.

Then she went to the cupboard and got out a box of special felt tip pens. Peter took out a pink one.

Peter began to draw his picture. He spent a long time
over it and took great care.

When he had finished, he showed it to his teacher.
She said it was very good.

Peter's pink panda

The teacher wrote a sentence underneath it in large letters for Peter to read. Then she pinned it up on the board for everyone to see.